Daniel Learns to Share

adapted by Becky Friedman

based on the screenplay "Daniel Shares His Tigertastic Car"

written by Wendy Harris

poses and layouts by Jason Fruchter

Ready-to-Read

Simon Spotlight

New York   London   Toronto   Sydney   New Delhi

SIMON SPOTLIGHT
An imprint of Simon & Schuster Children's Publishing Division
1230 Avenue of the Americas, New York, New York 10020
This Simon Spotlight edition December 2016
© 2016 The Fred Rogers Company
For information about special discounts for bulk purchases, please contact Simon & Schuster Special Sales at
1-866-506-1949 or business@simonandschuster.com.
Manufactured in the United States of America 1116 LAK
2 4 6 8 10 9 7 5 3 1
ISBN 978-1-4814-6752-0 (hc)
ISBN 978-1-4814-6751-3 (pbk)
ISBN 978-1-4814-6753-7 (eBook)

Hi, neighbor!

I am at the park.

I am playing cars
with my friends.

I show them my new car.

Honk! Honk!

Miss Elaina has a truck!

Wee-o! O the Owl
has a police car!

Prince Wednesday
does not have a car.

I do not want him to play with my car. It is mine.

Prince Wednesday is sad.

My dad tells us
how to share.

You can take a turn, and then I will get it back.

Now Prince Wednesday is happy.

My friends play with their cars.

I play too.

Vroom! Honk! Wee-o!

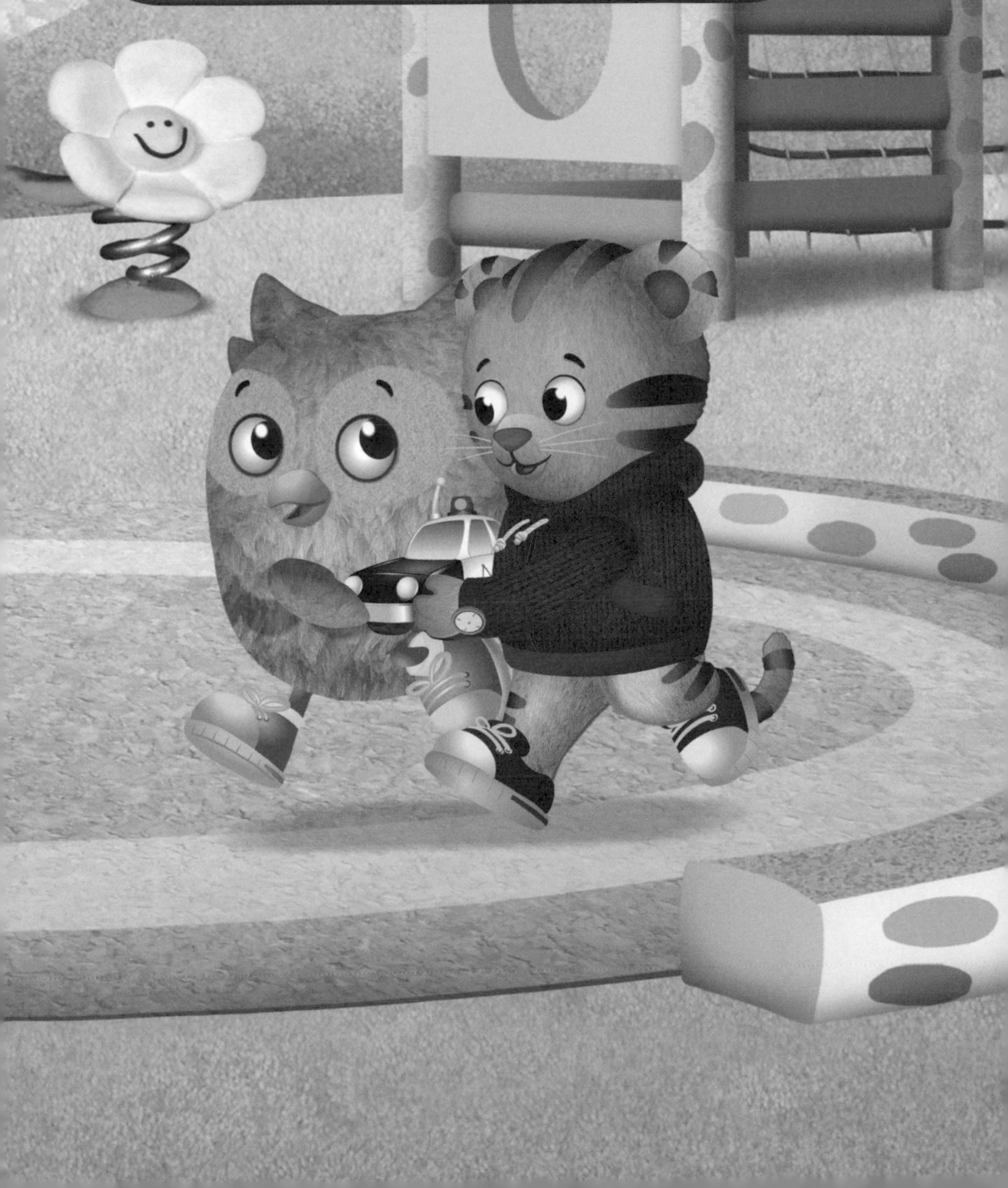

"Here is your car back," says Prince Wednesday.

"We can race our cars!" says Miss Elaina.

"I do not have a car," says Prince Wednesday.

"You can use my car!" says Miss Elaina.

You can take a turn, and then I will get it back.

What will Miss Elaina race with?

Miss Elaina uses a pretend car.

Ready . . . set . . . go!

Prince Wednesday gives the truck back.

Miss Elaina is happy.

Who will you share with?
Ugga Mugga!

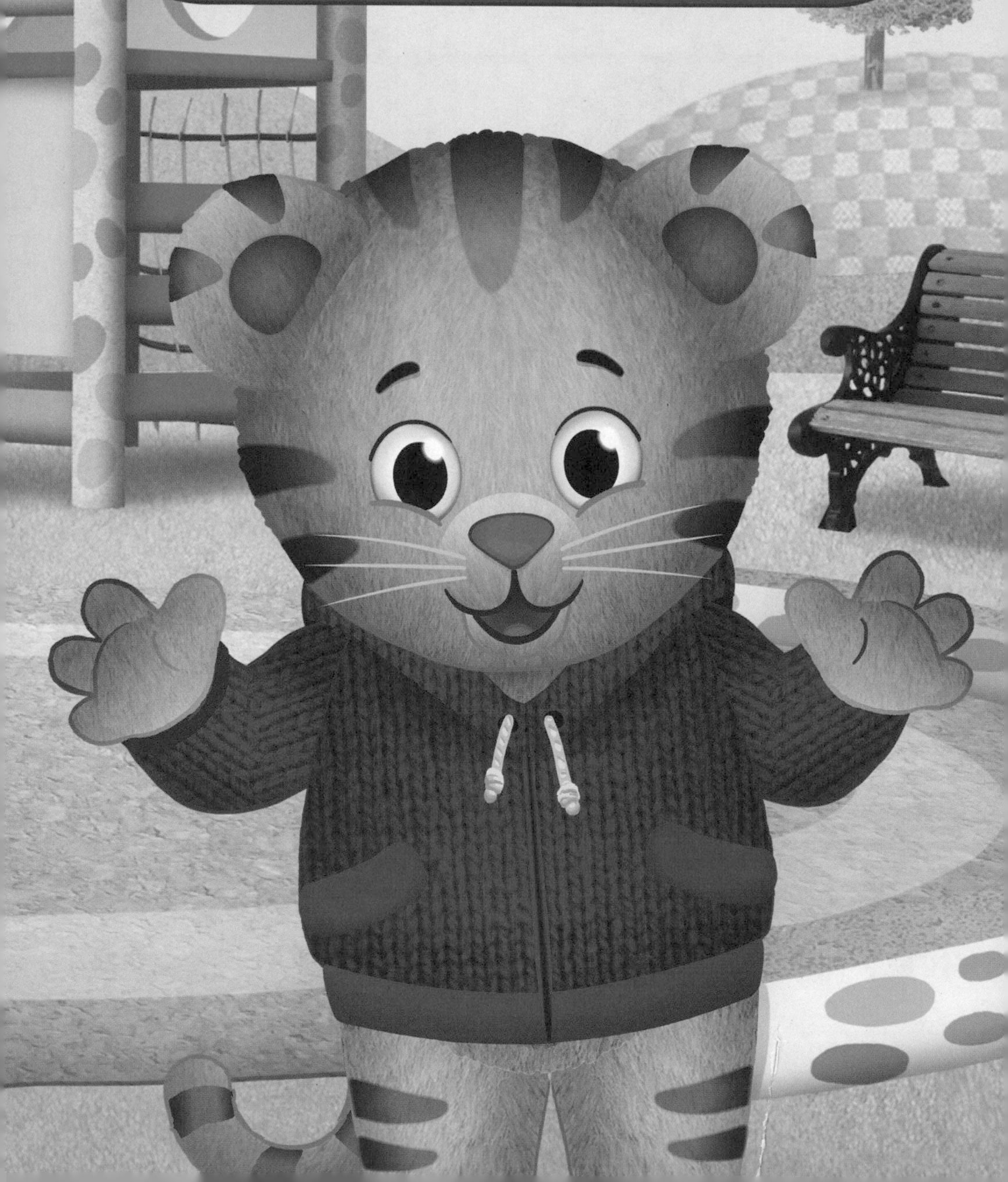